SARGASSO SKIES

THE SIX CROWNS

ALLAN JONES GARY CHALK

GREENWILLOW BOOKS
An Imprint of HarperCollinsPublishers

The Six Crowns: Sargasso Skies
Text and illustrations copyright © 2011 by Allan Frewin Jones and Gary Chalk

First published in 2011 in Great Britain by Hodder Children's Books, an imprint of Hachette Children's Books. First published in 2013 in the United States by Greenwillow Books.

The text of this book is set in Transitional 521 Bitstream.
Book design by Sylvie Le Floc'h

Library of Congress Cataloging-in-Publication Data is available.
ISBN 978-0-06-200636-3 (trade ed.)
13 14 15 16 17 CG/RRDH 10 9 8 7 6 5 4 3 2 1   First Edition
 Greenwillow Books

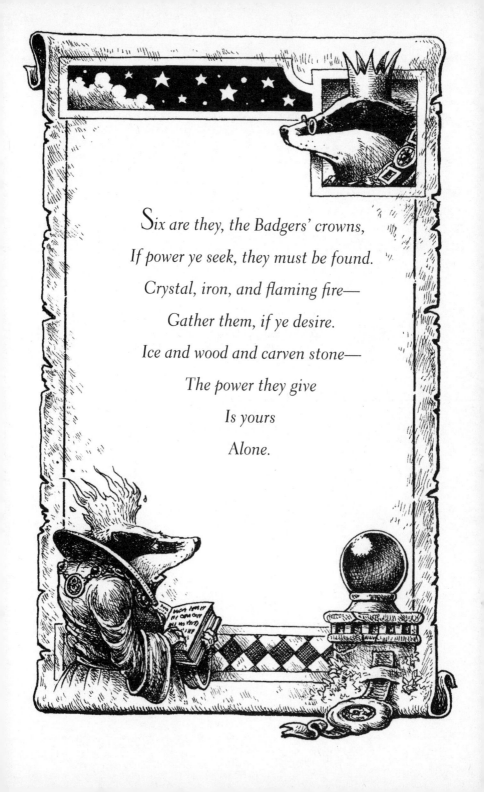

Six are they, the Badgers' crowns,
If power ye seek, they must be found.
Crystal, iron, and flaming fire—
Gather them, if ye desire.
Ice and wood and carven stone—
The power they give
Is yours
Alone.

❧ PROLOGUE ❧

The legends say that once, long, long ago, there was a single round world, like a ball floating in space, and that it was ruled over by six wise badgers. The legends also tell of a tremendous explosion, an explosion so huge that it shattered the round world into a thousand fragments, a vast archipelago of islands adrift in the sky. As time passed, the survivors of the explosion thrived and prospered and gave their scattered island homes a name—and that name was the Sundered Lands.

That's what the legends say.

But who believes in legends nowadays?

Well . . . Esmeralda Lightfoot, the Princess in Darkness, does, for one. According to Esmeralda, the truth of the ancient legends was revealed to her in a reading of the magical and ancient Badger Blocks—a set of prophetic wooden tokens from the old times. And her companions are beginning to believe it as well: reluctant hero Trundle Boldoak and light-hearted minstrel Jack Nimble are on the quest with her, and they've already found four of the crowns.

But there is a problem. Someone else is also hunting for the six crowns—his name is Captain Grizzletusk, and he's the meanest, bloodthirstiest, wickedest pirate ever to sail the skies of the Sundered Lands. And just to make matters even worse, Grizzletusk and his murderous pirate band are being helped by none other than Millie Rose Thorne, Queen of All the

Roamanys, and—horrifyingly enough—Esmeralda's very own aunty!

They have outdistanced their enemies for the time being and are heading for the mysterious island of Hammerland, where it has been prophesied that among the strange and sinister steam moles, they will find the fifth crown—the Crown of Wood.

But first they must navigate the dangers of the fearsome Sargasso Skies . . .

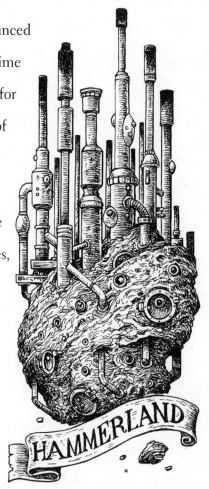

HAMMERLAND

1

TRAPPED!

"Oh, great, Trundle!" groaned Esmeralda. "Nice going. Now we're stuck!"

Trundle was on the narrow seat in the stern of the skyboat, red-faced and puffing with exertion as he tried to reverse the treadles that worked the propeller. "How is this *my* fault?" he gasped. "We were blown in here by a cyclone!" The wooden treadles were locked solid. He peered over the back of the *Thief in the Night*. Their little skyboat hung at an alarming angle, caught up high in the rigging of a wrecked windship. A length of thick, tarred rope had wound itself tight around the propeller blades.

"It *isn't* your fault," said Esmeralda. "But I have to blame someone, and you're nearest."

"Many's the windship has foundered in this dreadful gyre," Jack said, struggling to untangle himself from more rigging that had snagged over the prow. "I told you we might have problems getting safely past the Sargasso Skies." He pulled himself loose at last. "It's the graveyard of countless brave sky-faring vessels," he said mournfully. "Why, I could sing you sad ballads of lost and missing windships that would make you weep!"

"Later, maybe," said Esmeralda, sliding down the steeply sloping deck. "What we need right now is a sharp blade to cut ourselves free."

"Even if we do, we'll still be trapped in this awful place," Trundle said, staring unhappily out over the mist-shrouded wasteland of the dreaded Sargasso Skies. The desolation stretched away in all directions under dark and brooding clouds. This was without doubt the gloomiest and most dismal place he had ever seen. The rotting hulks of doomed windships rose like dark phantoms out of the crawling and swirling mists, their forecastles like ruinous towers, their masts poking up like broken fingers, their rigging hanging like wind-blown spiders' webs. And as if that wasn't bad enough, the air was thick with the stink of rot and mold and decay.

The sails of their gallant little skyboat hung limply from the mast, and their neat pile of provisions was now a higgledy-piggledy mess strewn down the length of the hull. The ferocious swirling winds that had dragged them off course had spat them out just as suddenly as they had sucked them in.

And things had been going so well till then.

They had sped away from the island of Spyre with

two of the crowns of the Badger Lords safely stowed aboard and with clear instructions about the next stage of their quest:

You must travel to the distant and sinister island of Hammerland and seek for the Crown of Wood among the steam moles!

The steam moles! Little was known about that peculiar and secretive race. The mysterious island of Hammerland was far away from all the main habitations and trade routes of Sundered Lands, out beyond a terrible place called the Sargasso Skies. And *that* was a notorious death trap they had every intention of avoiding.

"Steer well clear!" Esmeralda had told Trundle as the vast mist-shrouded reef of derelict windships and drifting debris had loomed up in the distance.

"Will do!" Trundle had responded, shifting the tiller accordingly.

Little did they know! The Sargasso Skies were at the center of a ceaseless swirl of turbulent winds.

Before any of them had time to prevent it, the whirling winds had taken the *Thief in the Night* by the sails and had dragged her into the heart of all the miserable wreckage. Out of control and spinning wildly, the hapless skyboat had come at last to a sudden jarring halt, trapped like a fly in a tangled web of rigging.

"We're never going to get out of here, are we?" said Trundle, shivering in the foul and chilly air. Although it had been clear daylight when the sky squalls had caught them, down here in the doldrums it seemed like perpetual night, the sky shrouded in a restless roof of dark clouds.

"Look on the bright side," said Jack, clambering laboriously up the deck. "At least Esmeralda's aunt Millie and those cutthroat pirates won't chase us in here!"

"I wish they'd try it," growled Esmeralda. "I'd love to see the *Iron Pig* smashed to little bits and all Captain Grizzletusk's bloodthirsty crew marooned here until they turn up their toes and die!"

"Just like we're going to do, you mean?" said Trundle.

"Now then, none of that!" Esmeralda said briskly. "Positive attitudes are what we need to get out of this mess. And the first order of the day is to cut ourselves free from all this old rope. Out with your sword, Trundle—get hacking!"

Trundle drew his sword and leaned out over the back of the skyboat.

Hack! Slash! Whack! Chop!

Trundle grinned as he worked away at the ropes looped around the propeller. It was good to see them splitting and falling away under his keen blade. This was more like it! This was proper hero stuff!

"Oops!" he said.

"What oops?" asked Jack.

"Why oops?" asked Esmeralda.

Trundle turned toward them, smiling nervously. "I think I got a bit carried away," he said.

Esmeralda put her paw to her forehead. "What

have you done?" she said, groaning.

"I sort of . . . accidentally . . . chopped off one of the propeller blades," Trundle admitted. "Silly me! Still, the propeller will work just as well with only three blades, won't it?"

"Of course it won't!" Esmeralda burst out. "It'll be off-balance. The moment you get going with the treadles, you'll twist the drive shaft like a corkscrew, you dim-witted animal!"

"Oh." Trundle felt terribly deflated. "Are you sure?" He looked hopefully at Jack, but the squirrel just nodded agreement with Esmeralda.

There followed a few moments of rather awkward silence.

"I don't suppose there's a spare propeller aboard?" Jack asked.

"You don't suppose right!" growled Esmeralda.

"Or something we could make a propeller blade with?" added Jack.

"We could try using Trundle's snout!"

"Wait a minute," Trundle said, rather alarmed by the way Esmeralda was eyeing his nose. "Isn't this whole place made up of smashed and wrecked windships and skyboats?"

"It is. What of it?" snapped Esmeralda.

"Surely there must be a working propeller out there somewhere?" explained Trundle. "Or at worst, some bits and pieces we could use to repair our own one?"

Jack's grin opened up like a piano keyboard, and he clapped his paws together. "Well done, Trundle!" he chirruped. "Of course there will be!"

"And tools, I'm guessing, to do the fixing with," Esmeralda chimed in. "And who knows what other useful stuff, as well. Nice thinking, Trundle!"

Trundle beamed at his two friends. From zero to hero in one leap!

"Well, don't just sit there grinning like a moonstruck oyster!" Esmeralda declared. "Let's get busy!"

"What about the crowns?" Jack asked, nodding towards the two boxes wedged under the stern seat—boxes that contained the mythical Crowns of Ice and Fire. "Should we take them with us?"

"I don't think so," said Esmeralda. "They'll be safe enough here. It's not like we're going far. With any luck, we'll find everything we need close by."

"That's as may be," said Jack, picking up his rebec and bow and slinging them over his back. "But I'm not going anywhere without my musical instrument."

The three companions made their way down to the front of the tilting skyboat. The broken mast of the windship that had snagged them rose up into the darkness. The remains of a powerstone basket could be seen where the mast had splintered.

"I suppose the powerstone must have floated away," said Esmeralda as she reached a leg out over the prow of the *Thief in the Night*. "I wonder what became of the sky mariners?"

"Best not to think about it," said Jack.

Esmeralda found a firm footing in the rigging and clambered slowly down into the white mist. Jack went next, and Trundle brought up the rear, his sword in his belt—just in case!

Trundle shuddered as fingers of mist crept in through his clothing and nasty putrid smells assaulted his sensitive snout.

"Ugh!" It was Esmeralda's voice.

"What?" Trundle called down.

"Oh, my!" Jack exclaimed.

"*What?*"

"I think we've found out what happened to the crew," said Esmeralda.

A moment later, Trundle reached the deck and saw what had upset his friends. Skeletons were strewn around the smashed and crumbling deck of the windship.

"Oh! How dreadful!" Trundle sighed, his gaze

drawn to the skulls, with their empty eye sockets staring out from among the sad little piles of bones.

Jack picked his way across the groaning deck and stooped to stare more closely at one of the skeletons. "I don't want to alarm anyone," he said. "But some of these bones have tooth marks on them."

Trundle shivered. "You mean they *ate* one another?" he stammered, more horrified than ever now.

"I don't think so," said Jack. "By the looks of the skeletons, I'd say this crew was mostly goats—but the gnawings aren't from goat teeth." He frowned. "They're long and pointy, like knives."

Trundle stared at the mysterious and threatening mists that crowded around the battered windship. "Do you think there could be cannibal animals living here?" he asked.

"The crews of wrecked windships turned wild and wicked by starvation and hopelessness, you mean?"

Jack intoned bleakly.

"Something like that," said Trundle.

"It's possible," Jack admitted.

"Then maybe we shouldn't spend too long standing around chatting," said Esmeralda. "Come on, Jack, let's look for some useful bits of wood and for tools. The sooner we're out of here, the better. Trun? You keep watch! If you see anything suspicious, give a yell!"

"You bet I will!"

Trundle edged nervously across the precarious decking, aware of every creak and crack in the sagging timbers. He came to the gunnels and leaned over, staring down into the murky depths.

He almost jumped out of his boots with shock.

Several pairs of luminous green eyes were staring back up at him. And at that same second, the air filled with high-pitched whoopings and hollerings.

Trundle leaped back with a yelp. "Fiendish

things!" he shrieked. "There are fiendish things climbing up the side of the windship!"

"What kind of things?" called Esmeralda.

"*Those* kind of things!" yelled Trundle, pointing to where the head of a large green lizard had appeared over the gunnels. The lizard's mouth opened. Its teeth flashed white and sharp, and its long black tongue flickered out. The eyes gleamed, hungry and ferocious. The creature gave a high call that was like nails scraping down a blackboard.

Another lizard head appeared. Then another. And another and another and another. And along with wide

mouths filled with knife-sharp teeth, Trundle noticed, the lizards clutched terrible weapons—great clubs and cudgels with iron spikes hammered through them.

"Run for it!" yelled Esmeralda.

Trundle zoomed across the deck as though he had been shot from a cannon. Yelling and screaming, the lizards swarmed after him.

"Jump!" shouted Jack.

Without any time for thought, the three friends threw themselves over the side of the windship. It wasn't a long fall, and they landed unhurt in a soft, boggy mire of rotten wood and oozy slime. Keeping close together, they waded through the stinking mess until they came to firmer ground.

"Now what?" gasped Trundle. The shrieking and calling of the lizards seemed to be coming from everywhere at once.

"That way!" said Jack, pointing to a thick bank of fog some way off. "They won't be able to see us in that!"

Nor we them, thought Trundle.

All the same, Trundle and Esmeralda chased the fleeing squirrel across the cheerless landscape of rotting hulks and quagmires. They raced over precarious planks that spanned great black holes—holes, Trundle guessed, that would send you plummeting down and down forever. They scrambled over uneven decking that crumbled at the touch of paw or boot. They leaped fallen masts and floundered through pools of stagnant oily water.

There was vegetation, Trundle noticed—plants that must have arrived here aboard stricken windships, plants strong enough and hungry enough to survive in all this desolation. Creepers and blobby mushroomlike things, and greeny-gray funguses and lichens, and odd-looking, evil-looking growths with ugly flowers and whip-thin tendrils that snatched at your legs as you ran past.

As they headed into the fog, they could hear

the lizards pursuing them, their long, clawed feet slapping and flapping as they swarmed smoothly over the debris, their eyes green as poison, their high calls echoing back and forth.

But then a different sound came to Trundle's ears. Not yelling and yowling. It was music! Distant organ music, echoing eerily through the mist.

"Do they seem like the type to play keyboard instruments?" gasped Esmeralda.

"No," exclaimed Trundle. "They seem like the type to bash you over the head and eat you!"

"Maybe there are survivors of the shipwrecks!" said Jack. "Maybe there's a camp or a town or something. Maybe that's where the music is coming from!"

This seemed to Trundle to be a whole lot of maybes, but he swerved as Jack swerved and the three of them ran full tilt toward the music.

They raced like mad things over the jagged and precarious terrain, but the music seemed to get no closer. Trundle began to wonder if they were imagining it.

"I recognize that tune," Jack said. "Whoever is playing, they're really good!"

"That's a comfort," gasped Esmeralda. "It'll be nice to listen to some well-played music." Her voice rose to a shriek. "While we're being *eaten alive!*"

Suddenly they came bursting out of the fog and found that they had stumbled into a deep valley with high, sheer slopes on three sides.

"It's a dead end!" wailed Jack. "Quick! Let's double back before they close in on us!"

But it was too late for that. Loping, spindle-legged shapes came looming out of the mists behind them. Green eyes flashed. Spiked cudgels lifted in long sinewy hands. White teeth snapped.

The three friends backed away from the approaching lizards.

There was no escape!

2

CHAINS

Trundle drew his sword and stepped forward, his knees knocking and his stomach in knots.

"Keep off!" he shouted, gesticulating with the sword. "Go back if you value your lives!"

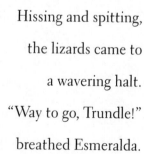

Hissing and spitting, the lizards came to a wavering halt.

"Way to go, Trundle!" breathed Esmeralda.

"Oh, well done, my lad!" added Jack.

Green eyes blinked and shifted as the lizards watched them, their backs bent, their arms hanging, their expressions uncertain.

"Advance on them, Trun!" urged Esmeralda. "Send 'em packing!"

Trundle wasn't so sure about that. He had just about used up all his reserves of courage. Those spiked cudgels looked nasty—not to mention the long, sharp teeth.

A particularly hefty lizard came barging up from behind the others, whacking a few of them over the head with his club as he did so. He glared at the three friends.

"*Spshhhspshhh?*" he roared, pointing at them.

"*Hiiisssssss!*" replied the lizards in chorus.

"Uh-oh!" said Esmeralda. "This doesn't look good."

"*Shrrrrraaaassssshhhh!*" bellowed the boss lizard.

"Leg it!" yelled Trundle as the whole mass of

lizards came surging forward, teeth bared and clubs raised.

Trundle and Esmeralda and Jack spun on their heels and ran for it.

But it was hopeless—even if they could outdistance the long-legged lizards, how were they to climb the sheer walls of the canyon?

Doomed! thought Trundle. After everything we've been through! I hope they're quick eaters!

They came to the far end of the valley. Using all four paws, they tried to scramble up the steep slope, but the ground was loose under them and they kept sliding down again toward the advancing lizards.

With a sinking heart, Trundle realized he had to perform another courageous act before it was too late.

He turned toward the lizards with his sword in his paw. "You two try to get away," he said resolutely to his friends. "I'll hold them off as long as possible. If you manage to find all the crowns and fulfill the prophecy, name a park bench after me or something!"

"Trundle, no!" gasped Esmeralda as he stepped forward to meet the marauding lizards.

The first of the lizards were only a few feet away when the air was suddenly filled with a weird, high-pitched wailing. It was a chorus of voices, singing as shrilly as birds, but with strange, unsettling harmonies and counter-melodies. And it seemed to be coming out of the sky.

The effect on the lizards was extraordinary. The foremost of them came to a skidding halt, jabbering and screeching among themselves and clearly disturbed by the eerie singing. Even the big boss lizard came to a stop and stared around uneasily.

"Lawks a-mussy!" gasped Jack. "Look! *Look!*" He was pointing up at the cliff tops that surrounded them.

The lofty ridges were filled with ghostly white shapes clad in white robes, and it was from the open

mouths of these spectral creatures that the singing was coming.

And even as Trundle and Esmeralda and Jack gazed up in astonishment at the spectral choir, the singing changed tone, and the melody rose to new heights.

That did it for the lizards. Throwing their hands up to the sides of their heads, they turned tail and fled, many of them dropping their cudgels and falling over one another in their rush to get away.

In a few hectic moments all the lizards were gone, swallowed up in the mist. And no sooner were the lizards routed than the piercing singing came to a halt, and a strange silence descended over the valley.

"Well now," breathed Jack. "That was curious, but I've never been so glad of a song in my entire life!"

"Who are they?" wondered Trundle. "*What* are they? Do you see their eyes?"

"I do," said Esmeralda. "Bright red eyes, every one of them." She frowned. "Jack, you've traveled all over the Sundered Lands. Have you ever seen the like before?"

"I have not," said Jack. "Very uncanny they are. Like phantoms."

"You think they're ghosts?" gasped Trundle. "I mean, I'm glad they frightened the lizards off . . . but I'm not keen on the idea of *ghosts*."

"We're about to find out what they are," said Esmeralda. "Here they come."

She was right. Many of the pale animals were making their way down the hillside toward them. Trundle stood his ground as the odd assortment of gliding creatures thronged around them. There were foxes and rabbits and pigs and sheep and cats and weasels and badgers and bears, all staring at them with their glowing eyes, all silent and all with perfectly white fur. They seemed especially fascinated by Jack's rebec, and many of them stared at it or touched it with cautious fingertips.

"Albinos," murmured Jack. "Well, I never! A whole tribe of albino animals."

"Hello there," Esmeralda said brightly. "You fellows just saved our lives with your singing. Thanks very much!"

The crowd of animals whispered among themselves, shifting and rustling restlessly, as though ill at ease.

Pleased as he was that these pale animals had come to their rescue, Trundle couldn't help but find them a little bit creepy.

"You sing very well," Jack said in a friendly voice. "I'm a musician myself, you know." He bowed low. "Jack Nimble, travelling troubadour at your service." He gestured to the others. "And this is Princess Esmeralda of the Roamany folk, along with Trundle Boldoak, a great hero." He smiled his widest smile. "And might I have your names, my good and worthy friends?" He looked from one to another. "Do you have names at all? Anyone?"

"Apparently not," murmured Esmeralda under her breath. "Do you think they even understand what we're saying to them?"

Suddenly, all the white animals turned to face the cliff at the end of the valley.

"Hello," breathed Jack. "Who's this now?"

A solitary figure stood atop the cliff, white against the brooding sky. Very tall and imposing he looked, with a mass of white hair and a great billowing white cloak drawn up to his face so that only the piercing red eyes were visible over it.

He held a long white stick in one hand, and he pounded it three times on the ground. The albinos gazed up at him with silent, reverential faces.

A deep, booming voice rolled down the hillside. "Ahhh! More able-bodied souls with the Great Endeavor to help!" The lordly shape turned and strode away. "Bring them!" he called.

A white rabbit turned to the three friends. "You

must come with us," the creature whispered.

"Um . . . we're jolly grateful for the rescue and everything," Esmeralda began. "But unless you tell us exactly who you are and what's going on here, we're not going anywhere with you weirdos, excuse my bluntness." She fixed the pale rabbit with a glittering and determined eye. "You'd have to chain us up first, matey!"

"Nice going with that comment about the chains, Esmeralda!" said Trundle, rattling his manacles.

"Oh, shut up!" Esmeralda retorted. "How was I to know they'd take me literally?"

The two hedgehogs were sitting together in a gloomy and grimy little room with curved wooden walls. They guessed they were aboard a wrecked windship. Somewhere deep below the decks, somewhere slimy and smelly.

No sooner had Esmeralda made her remark about chains than all the albinos had turned and fallen upon them. Before he knew it, Trundle's sword had been wrenched out of his hand and an old sack drawn down over his head. Then he was upended and the bag was pulled tight around his knees and he was lifted onto bony shoulders and carried off, with only Esmeralda's muffled cries of protest to be heard.

He had been jogged along for some time before he got the impression of being lifted up and then carried down to somewhere dank and stinky. The sack was taken off and the manacles were put on his wrists and ankles, and the gray shapes wafted away. A door clanged shut. In the deep gloom, he could see Esmeralda . . . but . . .

"What do you think has happened to Jack?" he asked.

"How should I know?" grumbled Esmeralda. "I've been inside a sack for a while, in case you didn't realize!"

She tugged at the chains, but they were attached

to a big iron staple that had been driven deep into the windship's timbers. "I could do with some food," she said. "Hey!" she yelled. "Jailers! Weirdos! Whatever you are! How about something to eat and drink around here?"

Trundle was just about able to make out their surroundings from the weak light that filtered in through the cracked and broken planks of the walls.

"Do you think they might have killed Jack?" Trundle asked.

"Possibly," said Esmeralda. "Or they might have just left him there to be eaten by those lizards. Who knows?"

"Or he could be chained up somewhere else aboard this old hulk!" Trundle groaned. "Being taunted and tormented by those dreadful creatures."

"I wouldn't be at all surprised!"

"Oh dear," moaned Trundle. "Oh, my!"

He was about to add, "Oh, calamity!" when he

heard the clinking of a key in a lock.

"Here they come again," growled Esmeralda. "Leave this to me, Trundle. I'll tell 'em what's what!"

Trundle looked unhappily at her. Telling them what's what had gotten them into this pickle in the first place. He dreaded to think what trouble more of Esmeralda's plain speaking might get them into.

The door swung wide.

"Hello there, you two!" said a familiar voice as Jack came into their prison bearing a food-laden tray in his paws. "I thought you might be a bit peckish!"

"Jack!" gasped Trundle in delight. "We thought *you* might be dead!"

"No," beamed Jack, grinning from ear to ear. "I'm not dead at all! In fact, I'm in the pink, my friends! I'm in the very pinkest of the pink!"

3

COUNT LEOPOLD

Jack gave the two captives a sympathetic look as he placed the tray on the floor between them. "You don't look too comfortable," he said. "It must be rotten to be imprisoned down here while there's so much exciting stuff going on."

Esmeralda gave him an irritated look. "It is!" she said. "And how come you aren't down here with us?"

"That's simple," chuckled Jack, lifting a mug to Trundle's lips and tilting it so he could drink. "I agreed to help Count Leopold." He picked up a hunk of bread. "Care for a bite?"

"What do you mean, you agreed to help Count Leopold?" growled Esmeralda. "Who is Count Leopold? And what exactly are you helping him do?"

"Oh, it's building and decorating work, mostly, at the moment, along with a spot of practicing," said Jack, popping a chunk of bread into Esmeralda's mouth. "I've joined the count's orchestra, you know. Second rebec, that's me."

"Is there any way you can get us out of here?" asked Trundle.

Jack tutted. "If you two hadn't been so uncooperative, you'd be a lot better off right now." He looked at Trundle. "You, waving your sword about, and Esmeralda being rude and sarcastic. I'm not surprised the count's people took offense."

"Would it help if we said we were sorry?" asked Trundle.

"It might," said Jack. "He's a decent sort of fellow, really. I think if you apologize and tell him you're willing to work for him, you'll be out of here in a trice!"

"Then we'll apologize," said Trundle.

"We won't!" insisted Esmeralda. "Tell him to release us right now! Tell him we have an important quest to be getting on with!"

"I will if you like." Jack sighed. "But if you insist on being stubborn, you'll be left down here permanently. And what about the quest then, eh?"

Trundle gave Esmeralda a stern look. "We will apologize," he said. "We will be polite and charming and pleasant. Won't we?"

"Yes," huffed Esmeralda. "Anything to get out of this putrid place!"

"Excellent," said Jack, getting up. "I'll go and tell the turnkey, and he'll let you loose." He smiled. "And then after you've eaten, I'll take you up to meet the count. You'll be impressed, I can assure you. He's quite a character!"

As Jack had promised, Trundle and Esmeralda were soon freed from their shackles. After a bite to eat, the merry squirrel led them up rickety stairs and along low walkways illuminated by candles set in iron sconces. Trundle got the impression that they were moving through a number of different wrecks, all knocked through and joined together. At last they came to a large pair of ornate carved doors.

Organ music filtered out from beyond.

Jack opened one of the doors a fraction and beckoned the others to follow him. They entered a long wood-paneled room lit by scores of candelabra. The music was much louder now—a frenzied, frantic tune that chased up and down the keyboards and shook the floor beneath their feet.

At the far end of the room, surrounded by clouds

of white mist, they could see a cloaked and wild-haired figure playing a mighty steam organ. Twisting and spiraling pipes jutted out from the back of the huge musical instrument, riveted together at odd angles, their joints wrapped in knotted rags and spouting steam and puffs of cloud.

The musician's hands rose and fell furiously, and his head tossed from side to side as he played. The music sounded odd and very complicated to Trundle. He liked music a person could tap his foot to. This sounded like music that might drive you out of your noodle if you listened to too much of it.

"The count plays brilliantly," Jack whispered as he led them along a moldy and ragged old carpet toward the shuddering organ and its berserk player. "He's a real master!"

"I wish he'd stop," mumbled Trundle. "It's giving me a headache!"

"Shhh!" hissed Jack. "He'll hear you!"

The frantic music came to a crashing climax and stopped. The organist's arms went limp, and he let out a long, deep sigh.

Jack cleared his throat as the last of the pipes ceased rumbling and the floor became still under Trundle's feet. "Count Leopold, I have brought you two new willing workers," Jack announced.

"And will they my bidding do?" growled the count, without looking around.

Jack gave Esmeralda and Trundle a hefty nudge, nodding toward the cloaked figure in its clouds of white mist.

"I suppose so," mumbled Esmeralda.

"Absolutely we will!" said Trundle, trying to sound enthusiastic even though the count gave him the collywobbles. "We're really looking forward to it!" he babbled. "We're just waiting for you to tell us exactly what you'd like us to do."

"And how long it will take," added Esmeralda.

"You see, we're on a bit of a quest, and . . ."

Her voice faded away as the tall, cloaked figure turned on the seat.

Trundle let out a gasp. Count Leopold was a lion.

Trundle had never met a lion, although he had seen pictures of them in books and had read descriptions of them that suggested they could be very dangerous—especially if you annoyed them.

Count Leopold's face was long and gaunt and haggard. Like the other animals they had met here, he was an albino, with pure white fur and with a white mane that exploded in all directions from his head. He stared morosely down at them, one of his fierce red eyes made oddly larger by a gold-rimmed monocle.

"You would know what task ahead of you lies?" said the count, his eyes glazing over. "I shall it you tell." His voice rose to a boom. "It is part of the greatest artistic endeavor to be the Sundered Lands ever have

witnessed!" He stood up, his cloak billowing, the mist swirling around his thin shoulders. Trundle found it a little tricky to understand exactly what the count was saying—he kept putting the words in the wrong places!

"You will assigned to a hulk be, and you will in the morning to work begin!" The count raised a paw. "Now, gone be! I have also work to do! Great music write does not itself!"

So saying, the great lion turned away and sat down again. His arms lifted, and a few seconds later the room was full of manic music.

Jack led Trundle and Esmeralda away.

"My opinion is that the count is a misunderstood genius," Jack said as they made their way back down the vibrating carpet with the organ music ringing in their ears.

"He's a misunderstood loony," said Esmeralda, staring back at the frenziedly playing lion. "That big white mane and those red eyes." She shuddered. "He gives me the screaming heebie-jeebies!"

Jack ushered them out of the room and closed the door behind them. Some of the silent albino creatures had gathered in the corridor, staring at them with their unfathomable pink eyes.

Trundle began to feel a little sorry for the strange animals. They seemed rather sad and forlorn in their long white robes, standing around like shreds of cloud that had lost the sky.

"Creepy creeps!" muttered Esmeralda as they passed through the ranks of the albino creatures.

"You might try to be a little more understanding of them," chided Jack as he led them away. "They can't help the way they were born."

"I'll be more understanding all right," Esmeralda remarked. "I'll understand them to pieces once we're out of here and back aboard the *Thief in the Night*."

"That might not be so easy," Jack said. "The

whole of Sargasso Skies is overrun with those nasty lizards. In fact, this is the only place they keep away from. They can't stand the music."

"I don't blame them," said Trundle. "It certainly gives me the willies!"

Jack frowned at him. "The count's music isn't easy, I'll grant you," he said. "But it's really wonderful, if you only give it a chance and really listen to it."

Esmeralda eyed him. "Ever heard the phrase 'Life's too short'?" she asked.

Jack shrugged. "Either way, you'd be crazy to try to escape," he warned them. "You'll get eaten for sure. Those lizards are as savage as savage can be, so I'm told!"

"So we're stuck here," said Trundle.

"I'm afraid we are," Jack agreed. "So you might as well make the most of it. That's what I'm doing."

"Yes, I can see that," said Esmeralda. "You've gotten yourself in with the count, all right."

Jack looked a little shamefaced. "I know it seems

like that," he said awkwardly. "But . . . well . . . I'm a musician at heart, you know. And the count really is an extraordinary composer and player, whether you realize it or not. He has a great vision . . . something entirely new and amazing that will astonish everyone in the Sundered Lands." He frowned. "Look, I have to be at rehearsals soon. I'll show you to your quarters. I'm told the hulks are quite comfortable, really."

"And where will you be sleeping?" asked Esmeralda.

"Oh . . . um . . . the orchestra has its own dormitory in the opera house itself. You'll see it in the morning. You'll be impressed, really you will."

Esmeralda gave Jack a deeply suspicious look. "I intend to get out of here at the very first chance," she said. "Will you be coming with us or not?"

"Of course!" Jack declared. "But until then, we should all make things as easy for ourselves as we can." He gestured for them to follow. "The workers' hulks are really very pleasant, so I'm told," he said.

"Come along. It's not far. There's hot food and warm beds."

"And is it out of earshot of that organ?" asked Esmeralda.

"It is," said Jack.

"Well, that's something, at least," she said. "Lead on, Jack, my lad. Lead on!"

4

THE
HERNSWICK
FLOTILLA

Jack led them out under the gloomy sky. While Trundle and Esmeralda had been chained up, night had fallen over the dire and dreadful Sargasso Skies. Broken-backed hulks wallowed all around them in the darkness, joined by a network of crisscrossing planks. Pale lights glimmered from portholes. Between the wooden walkways, the ground was oozy and unpleasant.

They came to a wreck with a rough doorway cut

into its hull. Jack knocked, and the door was opened by an elderly and very shabby frog clutching a flickering yellow candle.

The first thing that struck Trundle was the fact that the frog was not an albino; in fact, he looked to be a perfectly ordinary animal, except for his downcast features and his ragged and grubby clothing.

"Newcomers in need of a bed," Jack informed the frog. Then he turned to Trundle and Esmeralda. "Sleep well," he said. "I'll see you in the morning." Before they could reply, he pattered off and disappeared into the night.

"The name's Nigel Leaply," the frog told them in a voice so gravelly it made them want to clear their own throats. "But you can call me Hopper. Come on in. Keep your voices down—there's people in here what need their sleep."

Hopper led them into a long, narrow dormitory room lined with double and triple bunks, each of which contained a bundled-up and snoring form. It was quickly apparent, from the snouts and ears and tufts of hair that could be seen poking out of the blankets, that none of these animals were albinos either.

They tiptoed to the far end of the dormitory, where there were a few spare beds and where a saucepan of food was steaming on a black iron stove.

Hopper offered them tin bowls and began ladling out a thick and lumpy gruel. "Your mate the squirrel fell on his feet, all right," he growled. "The count is always on the lookout for more musical types for that orchestra of his." He gave a resigned shrug. "They get treated better than the rest of us. We all have to bunk in together and live on nothing but gruel, gruel and more gruel."

Trundle tried the thick gloop and was quite surprised to find it tasted better than it looked, although that wasn't saying much.

"What exactly is the count up to here?" asked Esmeralda.

Hopper eyed her thoughtfully. "He comes from the land of Umbrill," he began. "Of noble birth, by all accounts. But when he was born his folks didn't like the look of him at all—not when they saw how *white* he was. I don't blame 'em! They put him in a special kind of *home* and forgot all about him." Hopper picked a lump of something out of the gruel and chewed at it for a few moments. "He went off his nut, so they say—spent all his time writing music and playing the organ." He nodded solemnly. "He's a dab hand at that, I have to say, weird as he looks. Well," he continued, "long story short, he escaped from the asylum and nicked a windship and went sailing off all over the Seven Hundred Skies, searching for other animals who looked like him and who wanted to join up with him in his Great Endeavor."

"But why would he choose to live in such an awful place?" asked Trundle.

"He ain't here a' purpose," Hopper explained. "His windship got caught in the whirlwinds, just like the rest of us!" He shook his head. "Once in, there's no way out, chums." He gave them a curious look. "At least, not for the likes of us."

"And the Great Endeavor?" asked Esmeralda.

"He's writing a grand opera," said Hopper. "It just sounds like a horrible racket to me, but apparently it's very popular in some places . . . where people are more *sophisticated*." Hopper shrugged again. "Me, I like a tune you can dance to—something with a good rhythm."

"Me too," agreed Trundle.

"The steam moles are absolutely crazy for grand opera, apparently," Hopper continued. "That's why they're helping him."

"There are steam moles here?" asked Esmeralda in sudden excitement.

"A few of 'em," said Hopper. "They keep the steam organ running, and they're setting up a steam engine under the stage in the opera house to work a revolving platform and suchlike. And of course there's Alphonse Burrows—he's the bloke in charge of the steam moles' investment company. It's called Tunnel Vision Enterprises. Mr. Burrows and his associates have agreed to help the count for fifty percent of the profits, once the show goes on tour."

Trundle and Esmeralda looked at each another. This was the best news they'd heard since the sky squalls had dragged them down into this miserable place.

"How exactly are the steam moles going to help?" asked Esmeralda. "Do they have a way of getting out of here?"

"That they do," said Hopper. "They come here all the time in their strange iron windships, looking for flotsam and jetsam to take back home with them. Proper scavengers, they are. Their windships have steam-driven engines, so they can power their way through the squalls, unlike the rest of us poor souls." He gestured at the ranks of sleeping animals. "Some of us have been here for months and months," he said. "Sucked in by the winds and then attacked by those dratted lizards. Working for the count is no joke, I'll admit, but it beats being eaten alive!"

"But if the steam moles could get us all out of here, why don't they do it?" asked Trundle.

"That's 'cause they're waiting," Hopper said with a slow wink. "They don't do nuffin' for nuffin', if you know what I mean. They're waiting till the opera house is finished and the grand opera is ready to perform. Then they're going to send in a steam tug to tow the whole contraption off out of here." He waved his arms. "They plan on towing the opera house all over the Sundered Lands while the count and his company perform his opera to paying customers." He nodded. "It's all about the profit with them steam moles, you know. They might love Grand Opera, but the bottom line for them is hard cash."

"And how long before the opera house is finished?" asked Esmeralda.

"That's a tricky question," grumbled Hopper. "The way things are going right now—about twenty years, and that's a fact!"

"*How* long?" gasped Trundle.

"We're building the opera house out of scrap and debris," explained Hopper. "Except that none of us are architects nor nothin', so things keep falling down and having to be built up again. Proper dispiriting, it is."

Trundle was about to ask exactly how long they had been working on building the count's opera house, when a trapdoor burst open in the floor close to where the frog was sitting. Trundle gave a startled jerk, and a spoonful of gruel went flying.

The head of a shaggy, floppy-eared terrier dog appeared, topped off by a rather tatty military cap.

"Evening, Hopper, old boy," snapped the dog, emerging to reveal a frayed and threadbare army uniform. He gave Esmeralda and Trundle an appraising look and saluted smartly. "The commander wants to see the newcomers immediately," he barked.

"The name's Snouter, by the way. Lieutenant Snouter. Follow me!" And with that, the terrier dived back down through the trapdoor. Trundle and Esmeralda stared in astonishment at the dark hole.

"You'd better do as he says," suggested Hopper. "Best not get on the commander's bad side."

Snouter's head popped up again. "Come along!" he snapped. "No dawdling!"

"We may as well," said Esmeralda, wiping Trundle's gruel out of her eye. "It's not like we have any prior engagements."

The two hedgehogs slipped down through the trapdoor and followed the lieutenant through a series of twisting and turning underground tunnels, lit by small candles stapled to the walls.

"So, who is this commander of yours?" asked Esmeralda as they trotted along in Snouter's wake.

He replied without pausing or looking around. "He was the captain of our windship, the *Bellman*— part of the Hernswick flotilla. We were in convoy with the rest of the fleet, but we got lost in cloud and the Sargasso winds caught us. The commander got us off the wreck safely, but we were almost done for by those blasted lizard chappies. Managed to construct a redoubt and fight them off, although it was touch and go. Then we met up with the Count and his people. Rum-looking bunch, the lot of them, if you ask me. Hardly ever speak. Glum as the Goills. Uncanny, I call it. Anyway, we thought the count was one of the good chaps at first, don't y' know, but we soon discovered he's barking mad! Made us prisoners here, just like you chaps. But the commander is working to get us all out. And he'll do it, too—military genius, he is."

"Glad to hear it," said Esmeralda, grinning at Trundle. "This commander fellow could be our ticket out of here."

"Let's hope so," agreed Trundle.

Lieutenant Snouter came to a sudden halt under another trapdoor. He lifted a paw and began to knock.

Thump. Thump-thump. Thump. Thumpetty-thump-thump. Thump.Thumpthumpthumpthump-thump. Thump-thump. Thumpetty-thump. Thump.

He looked back at them. "Security, you know," he said. "You can't be too careful."

"Apparently not," said Esmeralda, hiding a smile behind her paw.

Lieutenant Snouter gave them a hopeful nod, peering up at the trapdoor every now and then.

"Maybe there's no one home?" suggested Trundle.

"Impossible!" snapped Snouter. "I'll give it another try." He was about to raise his paw again when a series of complicated knocks resounded from above.

Bonk. Bonk-bonk-bonk. Bonketty-bonk-bonk. Bonk-bonk. Bonkety-bonketty-bonketty-bonk. Bonk. Bonk-bonk. Bonk.

Snouter gave a single thump in reply, and the trapdoor was thrown open.

"Lieutenant Snouter reporting with the newcomers."

"Permission to enter," barked a voice. Snouter

vanished up the hole, swiftly followed by Esmeralda and Trundle.

They found themselves in a long, dark room very similar to the one they had just left. It was smaller, they saw, and it was inhabited entirely by various species of dogs, all wearing ragged and grubby uniforms.

A heavyset bulldog sat at a rough trestle table, apparently waiting for them. The chest of his jacket was covered in medals, and he wore a peaked cap with five tarnished gold stars around the brim.

He stood up and extended a solemn paw. "Welcome to Escape Central," he growled, his heavy jowls shaking as he spoke. "Under my command, the Hernswick Hounds are the only group in this whole benighted place working to escape."

"Glad to hear it," said Esmeralda. "What's the plan, matey?"

The commander gave her a stern look and

coughed in a disgruntled kind of way. Trundle guessed he wasn't used to being referred to as "matey."

"Take a seat and I'll tell you everything you need to know," growled the Commander. They sat opposite him while Snouter stood stiffly at their backs and the other dogs looked on from the crowded bunk beds.

The commander gave Trundle and Esmeralda a severe look. "We intend to get away from that Count Leopold fellow as quickly and as efficiently as possible," he said. "He's quite mad, you know." He gave them a rather stiff smile. "I'm sure two fine, upstanding young hedgehogs such as yourselves will do your duty and help us to escape."

"You bet we will!" said Esmeralda.

"You can count on us," added Trundle.

"Admirable!" said the commander. "Our plans are almost complete." He leaned forward and frowned at them. "You do have to understand one thing," he growled. "I'm in command here. We can't have people muddying the waters by making half-baked escape attempts on their own. We don't want the count put on the alert, you know."

"Fair enough," said Esmeralda. "By the way, have you thought of asking the steam moles for their help?"

"Impossible!" blustered the commander. "A chap can't trust them—not with those beady little eyes. Besides, they're in the count's pay. No, we prisoners must do this on our own!"

"So, what is your plan?" asked Trundle.

"Top secret!" growled the Commander. "Absolute security imperative!" He stood up again. "Good to meet you both. Know we can rely on you! Go back to your dorm now, and get a good night's sleep."

Esmeralda stared at him. "You brought us all the way here and now you won't even tell us your escape plan?" she exclaimed. "Are you crazy or what?"

"We'll meet again in the morning," said the commander, as though he hadn't even heard her. "All will be revealed then." He saluted. "Good work! Fine fellows! Ought to be in uniform! Don't know what you're missing!"

Before Esmeralda and Trundle had the chance to say anything else, they were bundled back down through the trapdoor.

Lieutenant Snouter's head popped through the hole. "You can find your own way back, can't you?" he barked. "Important military briefing taking place. Cheerio." The trapdoor crashed shut, and Trundle heard bolts being shot.

Esmeralda looked at him. "You know something?" she said as they made their way back to their own dormitory hulk. "I think it's a toss-up between the commander and Count Leopold which one's the barmiest!"

$\mathcal{E}$SCAPE $\mathcal{P}$LANS

It was not until Trundle and Esmeralda were led out the next morning at the head of a long column of miserable-looking captives that they became aware of the size and scope of Count Leopold's opera house.

The air was moist and clammy and the sun was just a blur through the thick hazy clouds, but there was enough light now to see the astonishing building in all its glory. Founded on a wooden platform supported by the hulls of several dozen windships, the great domed structure rose majestically out of the slimy swamps of the Sargasso Skies.

Externally, at least, they could see that it was all but complete. It was adorned with towers and columns and flying buttresses, and from its upper pinnacles, white flags flapped in the breeze. A host of powerstone baskets—presumably looted from crashed windships—were attached to the dome and to the highest towers, ready for the time when the Opera House would be lifted out of the mire and towed off by the steam moles to begin its grand tour of the Sundered Lands. Thick ropes and hawsers stretched down from the wooden platform, anchoring the opera house in place.

"Jack said we'd be impressed," said Trundle. "And he was right!"

From all the surrounding hulks, similar lines of

round-shouldered and tatty-clothed workers were making their way toward the opera house.

"Steam moles ahoy," murmured Esmeralda, pointing to an iron windship moored to one side of the huge building. Trundle nodded. Yes, that was definitely a steam mole vessel, with its dull iron pilot house and its great sooty funnel.

"And here comes the nutty commander," Esmeralda added. From another of the hulks, a troop of uniformed dogs marched smartly along behind their bemedaled leader.

Trundle gave him a wave, and the old bulldog snapped off a brisk salute.

"At least they don't look as downtrodden and pathetic as everyone else," Trundle whispered to Esmeralda.

"Hmmm," grunted Esmeralda, clearly not much impressed.

The lines of workers converged on the opera

house. Groups of albino animals stood at the various entrances, ushering the workers through and handing out sheets of paper. Trundle assumed they were instructions for the day's work.

Much to his surprise, as his column of workers plodded in through a side entrance, an albino bear pressed a sheet of paper into his paw.

"Er, I'm not the team leader," Trundle explained, trying to hand the paper back.

"They don't care," said Hopper. "Just read the instructions and we'll get busy." His voice lowered. "For all the good it'll do."

As they passed along a corridor, Trundle peered at the document. The instructions were very simple, and he read them aloud.

Work Team Seven

Lay Carpets in the Orchestra

Hopper began to laugh like a blocked drain after a thunderstorm. "I might have guessed!" he croaked, gulping in breath.

"What's so comical?" asked Esmeralda. "It sounds perfectly reasonable to me."

"It would," gurgled Hopper. "Until you realize that we spent all day yesterday fitting the seats in the orchestra—and now we're going to have to rip 'em all out again to lay the carpet." He shook his head, wiping a tear from his bulging eye. "What did I tell ya? Nobody knows what they're adoin' around here. We'll all be dead and gorn afore this here opera house gets finished, and that's a fact!"

"There's nothing especially hilarious about that," said Trundle. "What a total waste of time!"

"I know," chortled Hopper. "But you gotta larf, ain't ya?"

A few moments later, they emerged into the main auditorium of the opera house. It was chaos in there! Work teams were already hard at it, and the huge open space was full of shouting and yelling and banging and hammering and sawing and thudding and thumping. Ladders led up. Scaffolding teetered. Ropes dangled. Winches squealed. In one place, a bunch of workers were moving a great hunk of scenery while a second bunch ran after them, clutching ladders on top of which stood painters attempting to daub at the scenery as it was being moved.

Another group of creatures was hauling on ropes to lift a mighty chandelier up to the roof, while on the other side of the auditorium, a second group was hauling on ropes trying to bring it down again so they could insert candles. The chandelier jerked up and down, raining unlit candles.

Half of Trundle and Esmeralda's group ran forward and began to rip out the seats from the orchestra, while the rest got under their feet, attempting to unroll the carpet before there was enough space to do it. Hopper vanished under a great swath of carpet and work ground to a halt while they located him and cut a hole in the carpet to let him out.

As if this pandemonium wasn't enough, there was some very discordant music coming from the orchestra pit while a chinchilla on a podium, dressed in white tie and tails, clutched a baton and yelled furiously over the general hubbub.

"Tempo, gentlemen! Tempo!"

"This . . . is . . . crazy . . . ," Esmeralda intoned, shaking her head.

"It is a trifle disorganized," Trundle agreed. "Hopper was right—at this rate, the place will never get finished."

"There goes Sheila again!" came a voice from above, as a stoat fell screaming from a high gallery. She was only saved from serious injury because she landed on a big pile of curtains. Wiping her forehead and puffing out her cheeks, she scrambled off the heap and raced to a trembling ladder and began to climb again.

"Madness," said Esmeralda. "Utter madness."

"There's Jack," said Trundle, pointing to the orchestra pit, where their friend sat among many others, some albino, some not, peering at an open music score and sawing away at his rebec with his tongue sticking out of the side of his mouth.

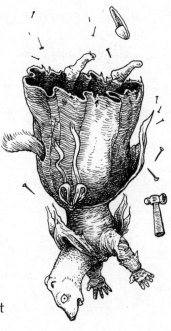

"He seems to be having fun," commented Esmeralda. "But those are the fellows we want to meet!" She pointed to the stage. There was a hole in the floorboards there, through which clanking and clonking and spouts of steam were rising. And standing at the front of the hole was Count Leopold, who was looming in a gangly way over a small, stout, important-looking steam mole in a floor-length black leather coat buttoned up tight to the collar.

"That must be Alphonse Burrows," said Esmeralda, pulling Trundle aside as a contingent of Hernswick Hounds went by at the trot, carrying a roll of carpet at shoulder height. They chanted in rhythm to their stamping feet.

> *"We don't know but we've been told—*
> *This carpet needs to be unrolled.*
> *We'll work when the commander calls*
> *And lay this carpet in the stalls."*

Trundle winced as the dogs crashed into Hopper's carpet-layers and a serious argument broke out. It ended when Sheila the shrieking stoat came plummeting down from the gallery again and bounced off the carpet roll.

"Let's go see what Moley and the Count are talking about," suggested Esmeralda as the reckless stoat raced by on her way back to the ladder again.

Skirting all the mayhem, Esmeralda and Trundle made their way up to the side of the stage. They stood half hidden in the wings, close enough to hear the two animals speaking.

"So far you have fallen three months behind schedule!" Alphonse Burrows was complaining, tapping at the blueprint spread out in front of them. "Our contract was for the maintenance of your steam organ, Count, not to mention the construction of a steam engine under your stage and the loan of a steam tug. We cannot make a return on our investment until work on this edifice is complete and the opera is ready to perform."

"Progress we are making!" insisted the count. "See you all the work that going on is!"

"Work?" grunted Alphonse Burrows. "All I see is

uncoordinated muddle and confusion, Count. The opera house should have been completed by now. And what of your grand opera? You promised me a finished score last week, but so far I have seen nothing and heard only dreadful caterwauling from your orchestra!"

"Caterwauling?" gasped the Count. "I'll you have know—"

But whatever he had been planning to say next was cut short when a large chunk of freshly painted scenery came crashing down, inches away from where the two animals were standing.

"What going on here is?" bellowed the count, hammering his stick down on the stage and glaring wrathfully around him. "Let us some organization here have!"

Animals invaded the stage from all directions, tripping over one another and occasionally plunging into the hole as they fought to try and move the fallen scenery.

"Ahem!" A growly
voice sounded from
close behind Trundle
and Esmeralda. They
turned and saw the
commander standing
in the shadows at
their backs. He moved
away, gesticulating for
them to follow. "Can't
be too careful," he
whispered loudly from
the corner of his
mouth. "Spies
everywhere.
Must keep the eyes
peeled. Not a word.
Keep close.
Top secret!"

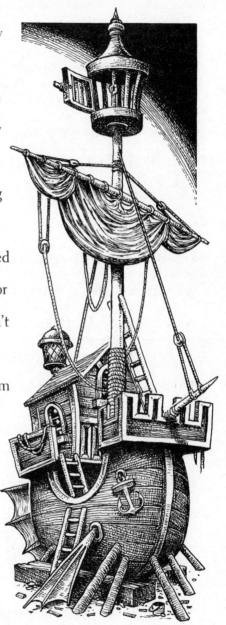

They came to a flight of steep wooden steps. The commander mounted the steps, moving ponderously and slowly, and puffing and blowing a great deal. Averting their eyes, Esmeralda and Trundle climbed up behind his rotund and tightly trousered rear end.

Up and up they went, high into the dusty and echoing vault above the stage, following narrow gantries and climbing tottering ladders until they were among the hanging and swinging scenery.

At last the commander pushed up through a trapdoor, and they found themselves directly under the opera house dome.

It was a few moments before the commander was in a state to do any more than sit down and suck in air and mop his face with a khaki handkerchief.

"Well I never," said Esmeralda. "Now that is *something!*"

Trundle had to agree that she was right. Almost

the whole of the space under the dome was taken up by a fully rigged windship.

"How did you get it up here?" gasped Trundle.

"Been working on it for months," gasped the commander. "My hounds have been carrying it up in small pieces. Top secret! Hush-hush! All done undercover. Sound of construction drowned out by the noise from down below." He seemed to have gotten his breath back now. He stood up, pocketing his handkerchief, and marched Trundle and Esmeralda proudly around the windship.

"Very nearly finished," he announced. "Then, all those workers who are with us will be let aboard in dark of night—and we'll sail out of here before the count and his followers can do a thing to stop us!" His eyes gleamed. "What do you say to that, eh? Impressive, or what? What?"

"I have two questions for you," said Esmeralda. She pointed to the mainmast. "The powerstone basket is empty," she said. "How do you plan to set sail with no powerstone aboard? And question number two—how are you going to get it out of here? The dome is solid—there's no way through!"

The commander frowned deeply at her. "Harrumph." He coughed. "That's all in hand, young lady. All information is given on a need-to-know basis, and you don't need to know, don't you know."

"No, I don't know," said Esmeralda. "That's the whole point. I'd *like* to know." She glanced at Trundle. "Because right now, your great escape plan looks like a total non-starter!"

"Non-starter?" exploded the commander, his face thunderous. "I say! Hold on there, young lady! I'm not used to being spoken to like that. Slip of a girl! Comes up here! Making comments to undermine morale!" His face was by now poppy red. "Never heard the like! Disgraceful! I'd court-martial you if you were one of my chaps! Dashed malcontent!"

"I'm sure she didn't mean to suggest you don't know what you're doing," Trundle said, trying to defuse the situation before the commander blew a gasket. "It's . . . er . . . it's a very nice windship indeed." He hooked a paw under Esmeralda's arm. "Come along, Es, we've got work to do. Let's leave the nice commander alone with his lovely windship."

"Yes, but . . ."

Trundle didn't give Esmeralda the chance to annoy the commander even further. He pushed her through the trapdoor and followed her down the ladder.

"It's a stupid plan," Esmeralda said, as they climbed back down to the stage. "Where are they going to get a powerstone from? And even if they manage that, and somehow get through a solid wooden dome without anyone noticing, there's still the winds to deal with. How are they going to get past them in one piece?"

"I have no idea." Trundle sighed. "But there's no need to antagonize him!"

"Excuse me, but there's every need!" grumbled Esmeralda. "He's a total loony and a complete waste of our time!" She paused at the head of the final steep stairway to the stage. "Listen, my lad," she said. "It's up to you and me and Jack to get ourselves out of here."

"How?" Trundle asked mildly.

"I don't know. Maybe we can convince the steam moles to help us after all. Come on, Trun, we need to go and talk to Jack." She winked at him as she began to climb down the steps. "Top secret, you know! Maximum security! Mum's the word!"

Chuckling to himself at her perfect imitation of the commander, Trundle followed her down into the unending chaos of the opera house.

6

ESMERALDA TAKES CHARGE

As they came down to ground level again, they heard a piercing shriek and saw Sheila go plummeting by into the orchestra pit. There was an odd *booomoiiinnnggg* sound, rather like a stoat hitting a drum. Sheila rose up again, her arms and legs flapping. She lost momentum and fell, accompanied this time by the sound of a drum skin tearing apart.

"My drum!" someone yelled. "Get her out of it!"

"Gurrrgh . . . urrrgh . . . wurrgh . . ." Sheila gurgled

as several pairs of helpful hands lifted her out of the broken drum and carted her off while the drummer sat by, his face in his paws, sobbing quietly to himself.

Trundle and Esmeralda made their way down to the side of the orchestra pit. Jack was there, the musical score spread out across his knees. He was perusing it with a furrowed brow while adding some rosin to the bow of his rebec.

His face cleared as he saw his friends approaching. "My, but this is good larks!" he said with a grin. "It's total mayhem, of course, and I can't make head nor tail of the opera the count has written. But it's such a treat to be among other musicians—I've really missed that, you know."

"Well, I'm glad someone is enjoying himself," said Esmeralda. "But there's still the Crown of Wood to be found, Jack! We can't stay here forever. I know we've outrun Aunt Millie and the pirates for now, but they're never going to give up looking for us. I'm sorry if I'm spoiling your fun, but we need to get out of this place as soon as possible."

"I agree," said Jack, unperturbed by Esmeralda's tone. "We were told to seek for the crown in Hammerland, were we not?"

"We were," agreed Trundle.

"Well, just take a guess where the first performance of the count's opera is due to take place?" Jack's grin stretched even wider. "I'll give you a clue. It begins with an H and ends in "ammerland"!"

Esmeralda gaped at him. "Truly?" she gasped.

"Absolutely!" nodded Jack. "First stop, Hammerland."

Esmeralda gave Trundle a slap on the back. "Didn't I tell you not to lose heart, Trun, my lad?" she declared, although so far as Trundle could remember she had said no such thing. "I knew the Fates wouldn't let us down!"

"So, if we stay with the opera house, we'll get taken

to Hammerland," said Trundle. "That's marvelous . . . if the place ever gets finished, that is."

"Hmm, good point," said Esmeralda. "Someone needs to take this lunacy in hand, and quickly, too!" She stared around herself, rolling up her sleeves. "Us Roamanys have been putting on shows and erecting big tops for five hundred years!" she announced. "I'll show 'em how to get organized." She fixed a determined eye on a crowd of goats failing to raise a timber beam. "And I'll start with *that* useless bunch!"

Trundle and Jack watched as she marched over to the fumbling creatures and started shouting orders. Within a few moments, she had sorted them into separate gangs, and it was not long before they had completed their task.

All around the auditorium, other animals were watching, and the moment the beam was slotted into place, a great cheer went up.

Esmeralda dusted her paws together and headed for the next bunch of workers.

Again, it was only a few minutes before order emerged from chaos, and another task was completed to general cheering and applause.

"Us next!" called other gangs. "Do us next!"

"She's astounding," breathed Jack.

"Isn't she, though?" said Trundle.

"It looks like the count thinks so, too," Jack added, pointing to the stage.

Count Leopold was staring at her, his monocle screwed tight into his eye. "Who is that woman?" he called.

Trundle was quick to scramble up onto the stage. "She's my friend Esmeralda," he told the count. "Scary, isn't she?"

"Totally on the contraryness!" declared the count. "She is wonderful! I appoint her my works manager as." He cupped his hands around his mouth. "Make so carry on, Ermintruda!"

"It's Esmeralda, mate!" she shouted back. "And don't you worry—I've got everything under control."

"Glorious! Truly magnificent!" said the count. He peered down at Trundle. "And what can you for me do, my little spiky friend?" he asked.

"Oh, I'm not really sure," Trundle stammered, feeling rather queasy under those strange red eyes. "I know all about lamplighting and . . . er . . . I'm a dab hand at cabbage soufflé . . . and . . . um . . . I do enjoy a good book . . . but . . . ."

"Ahh! A literary gentleman!" boomed the count. "Exactly you are the person who my papers a little organize can."

"Papers?" gasped Trundle. "Umm . . . what papers?"

"With me come!" With a sweep of his great cloak, the count led Trundle off the stage, poor Trundle needing to trot to keep up with the lion's long strides.

Off into the wings they went, and through a door and up a staircase, and through another door and along a corridor and this time up a spiral staircase. Through small windows dotted along the winding stair, Trundle could see that they were rising high above the swampy ground. He guessed they were in one of the towers.

The count came to a doorway at the top of the stairs. He flung it open and led Trundle inside.

Trundle found himself in a smallish circular room with curved windows and a pointed wooden ceiling. Filling the middle of the room and groaning under the weight of a vast disorderly mass of ink-stained papers was a solitary desk.

"This is my composing chamber," said the count. "Here are the words of my opera written—many words!" He put a great paw on Trundle's shoulder and guided him to a chair. "Sit!" he said. Trundle sat. "All that you to do I wish is the words of my opera put into the correct order," said the Count. "Such things to me are not of interest, but the people who to watch and to listen come, like a story in the right order told."

Trundle stared aghast at the towering piles of scribbled-on paper. There were even several dozen sheets strewn across the floor.

"I will have to you later on some food brought," said the count. "Until the task completed is, can you here sleep." He pointed to a straw mattress that lay against the wall. "It is most comfortable. You will sleep fast like a stone, yes?"

Before Trundle could say a word, the count swept to the door again. "A call you me give when you finished are!" he said. "I will you in lock so not disturbed will be."

The door slammed at the count's back. A key turned with a sharp *click*. There were the sounds of retreating feet on the stairs. Then silence. Trundle blinked at the door, and then at the mountain of papers.

"Oh, my!" he gasped, taking a sheaf of densely written pages from the pile. A small avalanche of paper slid forward, burying him to the knees.

"Oh, no!"

He blinked again at the closed and locked door.

With a deep, deep sigh, he brought the first sheet of paper up to his snout and began to read.

7

LEAPING LIZARDS!

All through that day, Trundle worked like fury among the count's papers. From below he heard the occasional thump or scream or thud or clank, and every now and then a high-pitched whistling noise that he assumed was something to do with the steam engine under the stage.

Twice, a silent albino brought him food and drink. Trundle was too nervous to say anything, and too busy with the papers to do more than take the odd bite and sip while the disorderly mass of the Count's opera began to make some kind of sense.

Night came, and Trundle lit candles and set them all around the floor.

"*Twilight of the Dogs,*" he muttered as he placed a final sheet of paper on the first of seventeen stacks. "Funny kind of name for an opera." He smiled as he regarded the fruits of his labors. "Not that I know anything about operas," he added. "But at least I've got it all in the right order, although whether an opera should have *quite* this many parts is another matter!"

Trundle was suspicious that if the count's entire story was performed, *Twilight of the Dogs* would last for several days!

Feeling a little drowsy, Trundle went to one of the small windows and pushed it open. He leaned out into the cool, murky night, breathing in the mildly stinky air, hoping it would keep him awake long enough to sort the few final papers still on the desk.

Fingers of mist coiled along the ground, sneaking between the dormitory hulks that lay below the tower. He looked up—and was surprised that from here he could see the faint glimmering of starlight through the clouds. The sight cheered him, reminding him of other, nicer lands out beyond the whirling winds.

There was a crash at his back, and a hearty voice called out.

"How's it going, Trun, my lad?" called Esmeralda. "I've brought you some cocoa."

Trundle stared as a draft of air snatched up the topmost layers of his seventeen neat piles and sent the pages swirling around the room like a startled flock of white birds.

"Arrgh!" he screamed. "Shut the door! Shut the door!"

"Oh! Okay. I'll leave you to it, then." Esmeralda placed the mug of cocoa on the desk, then beat a hasty retreat, slamming the door behind her.

The papers settled gently to the floor.

Trundle slumped down at the desk and banged his head a few times on the blotter.

Several weary hours later, Trundle placed the final sheet of paper on the final pile again. He glared at the door, daring it to open again. It didn't.

He was quite worn out. The small straw mattress looked very inviting. But first he tottered over to the window to close it and shut out the eerie Sargasso Skies night. He took a last glance over the sea of wreckage; it looked sad and gloomy in the weak starlight.

He was about to close the window when the sound of distant drums caught his ears. He stared out and spotted some long, thin figures scrambling about among the debris just beyond the farthest of the hulks.

He rubbed his eyes, thinking he recognized those stooping, gangly shapes.

"Lizards!" he hissed, alarmed to see the savage brutes so close to the opera house.

But there was something odd about the way the lizards were moving. Instead of skimming low along the ground as they had done when they had chased him and his friends, they were moving in long leaps and bounds. And each of them was clutching a largish bundle in its arms.

"How odd," he said aloud. He yawned, tired to the bone and far too sleepy to know what to make of what he was seeing.

"I hate those lizards," he grumbled, shutting the window and firmly turning the latch. Half asleep on his feet, he stumbled across the room and was snoring almost before he hit the mattress.

❧ ❧ ❧

He awoke early the next morning and for a moment wondered where he was. Then he remembered.

"Twilight of the Dogs!" he muttered to himself, sitting up and knuckling his eyes. "And today I'm going to try and make some sense of the story . . . if it *has* any sense to it!"

Truth be told, Trundle was almost enjoying himself among the count's teeming papers. There was something oddly satisfying about creating order out of all that chaos, and he had even discovered in the desk a pen and an inkpot and some sheets of blank paper on which he made notes in his large, round handwriting.

He had lost track of how long he had been working when he heard a soft rustling sound at his back. He turned and saw that a silent albino rabbit had slipped in through the door, carrying a tray that held a steaming cup of tea and a plate of glazed buns.

He blinked uneasily at the red-eyed creature as it

glided forward and placed the tray on the corner of the desk.

"Thank you very much," Trundle said.

With a slight nod, the albino rabbit turned to leave.

"I say," Trundle added. "How are things going downstairs? Esmeralda's got them all jumping, I bet!"

The white face remained blank, but the red eyes widened as the rabbit moved to the door and slipped through quickly.

Trundle frowned after the pale creature. "You know something?" he said out loud to himself. "I sometimes get the impression that those animals are more frightened of us than we are of them."

Trundle spent another entire day up in the tower room. But he had the feeling that his labors had not been in vain. Lighting candles as the evening darkened, he walked slowly around the desk. The seventeen original piles of paper had been reduced to three; the discarded writings heaped like a snowdrift against the wall.

Twilight of the Dogs was starting at last to work as a story. And Trundle found that it wasn't such a bad story, after all. There was plenty of action, with swordfights and fearsome dragons and kings and queens and evil monsters and dastardly schemes and handsome imperiled heroes and beautiful gallant princesses who rode about on unicorns to save them.

He stretched and yawned. "I must be the only silly soul awake in this entire place!" He sighed, rubbing his red-rimmed eyes.

Yawning, he opened the window, remembering the drums and the lizards from the night before. Would they be there again? he wondered. And if so, what were they up to? Nothing good, he felt sure of that.

He heard the faint boom of the drums. Maybe it was some kind of communication system among the lizards?

"Like someone banging a gong to let you know it's dinnertime," he said with a shudder. "And there they are again!"

Sure enough, a band of lizards was bounding along clutching wrapped-up bundles—moving in the same weird way as they had the previous night.

But then something else took his attention. A large hatch opened among the debris, close to the back of one of the hulks. The heads of several dogs appeared. They scrambled out, and Trundle saw that they were all dressed in military uniforms.

"It's some of those Hernswick Hounds," Trundle mused aloud. "I suppose the commander has his soldiers patrol the perimeters, just to be on the safe side!" He frowned. "Those lizards are in for a bit of a surprise! There'll be a big punch-up now, and no mistake!"

As Trundle watched, the lizards bounded closer to where the dogs were gathered. There were about

as many hounds as there were lizards. Trundle bit his lip—this was going to be nasty!

But to his amazement, the two groups met face-to-face without so much as a single punch being thrown or a single tooth being gnashed. Trundle stared in puzzlement as the lizards calmly handed their bundles over to the hounds. Almost immediately the hounds zipped back down through the hatch and closed it behind themselves.

Then the lizards turned tail and went scuttling off until they vanished into the creeping mists. But they were no longer leaping and bounding—they were moving along quite normally.

Trundle closed the window and went and sat on his mattress. This needed thinking about!

Despite feeling so sleepy, he racked his brains, trying to understand what he had just seen.

Suddenly he snapped his fingers. "Got it!" he crowed. "Those bundles must contain scraps of powerstone—that's why the lizards were leaping along like that. The buoyancy of the powerstone made them much lighter. Somehow the commander has done a deal with the lizards—and he's using them to collect enough powerstone to fly his windship!"

Of course. That made perfect sense.

One thing troubled Trundle as he stretched himself out on his mattress with his arms behind his head.

"I can see what the commander is getting out of the deal," he said to the pointed ceiling. "But what's in it for those darned lizards? I can't imagine them helping the commander out of the kindness of their hearts." His eyes narrowed. "I wouldn't trust them, that's for sure!" he said. "I wouldn't trust them in a million years!"

Trundle was awakened by a rough paw shaking him by the shoulder and by a horribly cheery voice chirruping in his ear.

"Come on, you slugabed!" Jack said. "I've brought you a cup of tea with an optional bun!"

Trundle sat up, glad to see his friend despite the boisterous nature of the merry squirrel's wake-up call.

He rubbed his eyes and yawned. "How's it going down there?" he asked.

"Esmeralda has worked miracles," Jack said. "Things are very nearly finished on the stage and in the auditorium. It looks a treat." He sat down with a sigh. "But the music is a real problem. It's wonderful stuff, but there's so much of it. It goes on forever, and I can't make ears nor tail of the plot of the opera—if it even has one!"

"Ah, but it does!" said Trundle. "It's been hard work, and I had to get rid of some truly awful stuff—mostly to do with people moping about because they're in love with other people who are in love with someone else. Really ghastly! There were pages and pages of it." He pointed to the heap by the wall. "I dumped the lot! I can't stand that whiny smoochy drivel."

"And is the rest any good?" asked Jack.

"Surprisingly, it is," declared Trundle. "Very good, most of it, now I've got the whole thing in the right order. Count Leopold writes like he speaks—with everything back to front and inside out and upside down!"

"But you sorted it?"

"I did," Trundle said quite proudly, gesturing toward the single neat stack of papers left on the desk. "It's rather exciting, actually." He frowned. "I just hope the count will agree with the cuts and the changes I've made." He stood up and trotted over to the desk, where several spread-out sheets of paper were pinned together on the blotter. "Look," he said. "I've made a flowchart of the acts and scenes, showing where they ought to come and how the whole story should work."

"Amazing!" said Jack, leaning over the chart. "Ahh! I see. Yes. It makes perfect sense to have Bruinhilda's aria there, leading into the battle between the bad dogs and the noble bears. And there's the 'Ride of the Volekyries'—that's got a really good bit of music to it! Stirring stuff. And you've put the coronation of the king right at the end, just where it ought to be!" Jack slapped Trundle on the shoulder. "You're quite the editor, my lad." He beamed. "This is splendid work!"

Without any warning, two huge white paws came clamping down on their shoulders. If the weight hadn't held him down, Trundle might well have leaped clear out of his prickles with the shock.

"It is splendid, indeed!" boomed the count. "This here is my most wonderful work! With it, will I tour the Worlds!"

And with that, the count reached past them and grabbed up the chart and the pile of papers that represented the fruits of all Trundle's labors.

Twilight of the Dogs

An Epic Opera in Three Acts

Words and Music by Count Leopold of Umbrill

"Excellent, excellent," said the count, striding to the door and disappearing through it. "A genius am I!"

"It drives me crazy, the way they can creep up behind you without a sound," said Jack. "How do they do that?"

Trundle stared after the vanished count. "Thanks for all your help, Trundle," he murmured under his breath. "I couldn't have done it without you, Trundle." He sighed. "Oh, don't mention it, count. It was my pleasure!"

Roaring with laughter, Jack slapped him on the back. "Never you mind, Trundle old lad," he said. "Editors never get the appreciation they deserve!"

8

FIRE!

Jack and Trundle descended from the high tower room and came out into the auditorium. The transformation that had taken place in the opera house was amazing. Order had been created out of chaos. The place looked almost ready for an audience to arrive and take their seats. Brightly painted scenery was being moved into position on stage, and around the walls, animals on carefully held ladders were gilding a final few ornaments and polishing up the last of the woodwork. Trundle was also quite pleased to see Sheila the stoat, up near the ceiling, looking none the worse for wear, hooked into a safety harness and roped up to two stout bears, flicking with a feather duster at the huge chandelier.

Esmeralda was sitting midstage on a papier-mâché throne, checking props and costumes that were being presented for her approval by an orderly procession of albino animals. Beneath her feet was the completed revolving stage, from under the edges of which spouted the odd wisp of steam and from beneath which echoed the odd clank, rumble, and clang.

Trundle and Jack approached their friend. "Hmmm," she was saying to a raccoon who was standing patiently at her side with several glittery props in his arms. "The silver paper on the crown looks fine, Rocky, but you need to give the orb a bit of a polish." She clapped her hands. "Everything else looks perfect. Well done, everyone!" She spotted

Trundle and Jack and grinned at them. "Hello, boys," she said. "The count came bounding down in great spirits a few moments ago shouting that 'It is all in best order and finished.'" She pointed down to the orchestra pit. "He's busy giving his instructions to the conductor. Looks like you did a first-rate job there, Trun."

"You, too," said Trundle, gazing around admiringly.

"I seem to have a natural talent for motivating people," said Esmeralda.

"Yes, it's called being a bossyboots." Jack grinned.

Esmeralda stuck out her tongue at him and then laughed.

Trundle was gazing down into the orchestra pit. The chinchilla conductor was standing on his tall plinth in his tail suit and white tie, nodding and pointing while the count loomed over him. Trundle's opera chart was spread on the podium, and the count was talking rapidly and making wide gestures with both arms.

"Have you it, mousetro?" asked the count.

"You go too quick!" complained the conductor.

"But have you it, yes?"

"Yes, yes, I have it!"

"Then is all good!" boomed the count, straightening up and letting his voice roar out through the opera house. "Wonderful is it all! At two o'clock this afternoon will there be dress rehearsal! Last touches finish, and then for lunch will everyone break."

A few busy hours later Esmeralda, Jack, and Trundle were sitting quietly together at the side of the stage, their legs swinging as they nibbled their gruel sandwiches. All over the auditorium, worn-out animals were also having a well-earned break.

"This stuff is just awful," moaned Esmeralda, putting her sandwich aside and making a disgusted face.

"Really?" said Trundle, eating appreciatively. "I was thinking it reminds me of home."

"It would." Jack sighed, chewing slowly. "It tastes like week-old cabbage!"

"I think we should have a quick word with the commander," said Esmeralda, nodding over to where the fat old bulldog was sitting in a circle of his Hernswick Hounds. Trundle had told her all about the nocturnal activities of the soldier dogs and the lizards, and she was determined to find out whether he had guessed correctly.

The three friends headed over to the ring of dogs and stood at the commander's side.

"We know where you're getting your powerstone from," Trundle said in a low voice. "I saw your people and the lizards together last night."

The Commander frowned at him. "Fine chaps, those lizards," he barked. "They're a bit of a rabble, but show 'em some authority and they soon rally round the flag, don't you know. Meek as dormice. Most obliging fellows."

"And have they given you enough powerstone to fly out of here yet?" asked Jack.

The commander's voice dropped to a conspiratorial whisper. "Last night was the final consignment," he hissed. "All in order. Final checklist and we're off. Splendid job! First rate!"

"You still haven't told us how you plan on getting the windship out from under the dome," said Esmeralda.

"Aha! That's all in hand, young lady!" said the Commander. "We've been systematically weakening the roof beams over the past weeks. Sawing through 'em, don't you know. All carefully planned. When the 'Ride of the Volekyries' reaches its crescendo, my most reliable hounds will make their way up to the dome and saw through the remaining supports. The dome has powerstone attached. It'll simply float away! Then we get everybody aboard, and sail off! Mission complete!"

He eyed them suspiciously. "You've been collaborating with the enemy," he growled. "Bad show! But you helped to keep that nutty old Lion busy while we finished our work—so there are places on the windship for the three of you, if you're interested."

"How do you plan on getting through the whirlwinds up there?" asked Jack.

"No problem!" declared the commander. "Expert navigators aboard. Excellent windshipmen. They'll find a way through. Absolutely!"

"You mean the same excellent navigators who got you marooned here in the first place?" said Esmeralda. "I see." She turned to Trundle and Jack, twirling her fingers at the side of her head and going cross-eyed.

"And if you *do* break through, where will you be heading?" asked Trundle.

"Back to Hernswick," snapped the bulldog. "Reporting for duty! Imperative I explain absence from the flotilla. Court-martial otherwise!"

"So you wouldn't be going anywhere near Hammerland, then?" asked Trundle.

"Rather not!" said the Commander. "Totally wrong direction! Needed back at base. Absent without leave. Must report to the high command."

"In that case," Esmeralda said, "good luck with the winds, matey. We won't be coming with you." She patted him on the shoulder, mimicking his way of speaking. "But jolly good luck, old chap! First rate and all that! Spiffing! Absolutely spiffing!"

She turned and walked away from the goggling hounds and their spluttering commander. "Come on, boys, we're done with these loonies! We'll stay with the count and hitch ourselves a free ride to Hammerland."

"Extraordinary!" huffed the commander. "Young women these days! Absolutely extraordinary!"

❦ ❦ ❦

Esmeralda and Trundle found themselves a couple of good seats in the front row. It was almost two o'clock. The curtain had been drawn down, hiding the stage. The orchestra was tuning up, and a sense of anxious anticipation filled the auditorium.

Sitting silently all around the two friends was a delegation of steam moles, all in long black leather coats, all wearing thick glasses and all writing things down in spiral notebooks. Congregating in the other seats were all the animals who had worked so long and hard to get the opera house ready for the grand dress rehearsal.

Down in the orchestra pit, Jack sat among the other musicians, all of them taking a last look at their musical scores, warming up their instruments, and waiting for the mousetro to give the sign that meant everything was ready for the overture to begin.

There was no sign of Count Leopold, but

occasionally his voice could be heard booming out from behind the curtain.

Then . . . at long last . . . an expectant silence descended.

The mousetro beat his baton thrice on the podium.

Tap. Tap. Tap.

The music began, starting low but then swelling up like rising floodwaters, filling the entire auditorium with sound as the melody grew and grew.

"Blimey!" hissed Esmeralda, leaning close to Trundle. "This doesn't sound half bad after all!"

"Shhhh!" hissed a dozen steam moles.

Trundle stared around himself with his mouth half open. He was tingling with nervous excitement all the way from his spiky head to his furry toes. He was about to hear, for the first time, the opera he had been working on solidly for the past three days! Would anyone like it? Would it get booed? Would the count blame him if it fell flat? He crossed all his fingers and toes, his heart palpitating.

The curtain rose to reveal a landscape of purple mountains under an orange and flame-red sky. In among the saw-edged mountain peaks stood the ancient fortress of Bruinhilda, warrior maiden and formidable champion of the noble bears of Volehalla.

As the music reached a frenzied climax, the hefty, armor-clad albino bear playing Bruinhilda strode to center stage. She came to a halt, her armor shining in the light of a row of candles set in small metal cups along the front edge of the stage. She threw back her yellow braids and lifted her sword.

"Well, look at that!" gasped Trundle, staring at the sword in Bruinhilda's big white paw. "I wondered where that had gotten to!" It was his own sword, being used as a prop in Count Leopold's opera.

Fancy that! he thought, rather liking the idea. At least I'll know where to find it if I need it.

Meanwhile, Bruinhilda took in a deep, bosom-expanding breath and opened her mouth to sing the opening aria of the first act of *Twilight of the Dogs*.

But then Trundle saw her eyes almost pop out of her face as she goggled in astonishment at something that was evidently taking place at the rear of the auditorium.

A moment later she gave a high-pitched shriek. "Lizards!"

Esmeralda leaned close to Trundle. "I didn't know there were lizards in the opera," she whispered.

"Shhhh!" hissed a dozen steam moles.

"There aren't!" said Trundle with a dreadful sinking feeling.

"Lizards!" howled Bruinhilda again, pointing over everyone's heads. "Lul-lul-lul-lizards! Blooming millions of them!"

Everyone turned and everyone saw, and suddenly everyone was also yelling and screeching, "Lizards! Lizards!"

And they had good reason! For streaming in through the wide-open doors at the rear of the auditorium was a whole army of cudgel-wielding lizards!

Even though they were taken by surprise, many of the animals seated in the opera house managed to grab something to fight back with. They stemmed the flow of hissing lizards, battling them with hammers and wrenches and leftover pieces of wood and metal—not to mention the occasional ripped-up chair and handy ladder.

A bunch of albino animals came rushing from backstage, singing the same eerie song that had driven the lizards away before. But the lizards took no notice. It was almost as if—

"They have earplugs!" yelled Trundle. He gestured wildly to the singers. "It's no good! They can't hear it! You have to fight!"

And so saying, he leaped up onto the stage and

snatched his sword out of Bruinhilda's grip. "Sorry," he said. "I need it back." He brandished his sword angrily at the Commander, who was busy barking orders to his hounds.

"This is all your fault!" Trundle raved at him. "Those lizards were just using you to find out where all your tunnels were! It was their plan all along to sneak in here and eat the lot of us, you nincompoop!"

"I say," growled the affronted bulldog. "Steady on there, old chap! Unforeseen circumstances! Seemed decent enough fellows! Dashed turncoats, every one of them!"

"Yes, they are!" howled Esmeralda. "So start fighting them, before it's too late!"

The commander glared at her for a moment. Then an iron-spiked cudgel went whistling past his ear, and he decided not to care so very much about women giving him orders.

"Hernswick Flotilla!" he roared. "Grab any weapons you can, men! By the left—*chaaaarge!*"

It was an absolute uproar in the auditorium, with whacks and thuds and yells and howls echoing to the ceiling as the lizards clashed headlong with the worker animals. Combatants on both sides went tumbling over the chairs as the battle raged.

The Hernswick Hounds thundered up the center aisle in formation and crashed into a whole swarm of lizards coming the other way.

Esmeralda led a bunch of musicians out of the orchestra pit, wielding violins and trumpets and bassoons and flutes as they hurled themselves into the fray.

Jack's rebec came down on a lizard's head, flattening it into the carpet.

"One down!" he shouted. "Two hundred to go!"

Trundle was about to leap into the melee when he heard a booming voice at his back.

"Fire they like not!" shouted the count, racing across the stage with a tall candelabra in his paw. "We must on them fire use!"

Trundle snatched up one of the candlesticks that lit the front of the stage and jumped down into a milling bunch of lizards. The effect of the candle flame, coupled with his slashing sword, was all that he could have wished for.

Hissing and squealing, the lizards scrambled to get away from him.

He saw more animals—including many albinos— grab up candles and race forward, beating the lizards back, until half the auditorium was clear of them again and the doors were blocked solid with lizards trying to escape.

Swept up in the general chaos, it was difficult for Trundle to tell exactly what was going on—but it was clear that the defenders were slowly gaining ground on the spitting and shrieking lizards.

Suddenly he found himself outside the opera house, fighting a lizard who was making a last stand on the edge of the wooden platform. All around him he could see animals brandishing newly lit flaming torches. The flickering red flames made even more of an impression on the lizards than the candles had. The cowardly creatures leaped from the platform and scuttled off across the mire, weeping and wailing that their intended meal had fought back so hard.

Trundle turned, waving his sword. "Victory!" he yelled. "Yay, us!" But then he saw that several torches and candles had been dropped during the fight, and that fires were leaping up all over the platform.

"We're on fire!" he howled. "Quick! Put them out! The whole place will burn to the ground!"

With the lizards in full retreat, the defenders turned their attentions to the fires—but in several places the flames were licking high up the opera house walls, far beyond anyone's ability to stamp them out.

"Cast off the ropes!" shouted Esmeralda. "Set the opera house adrift before the whole place goes up in flames!"

Animals raced to the hawsers holding the opera house in place. Tools were snatched up, saws and knives and pincers and anything else with a sharp edge. Trundle even hacked away with his sword.

One by one the thick ropes were severed.

"Back inside!" shrieked Esmeralda. "Get into the building, or you'll be left behind!"

The opera house groaned and creaked as the animals came flooding in through the entrances. Just as the last foot of the last animal left the burning platform, the opera house broke loose and slowly lifted into the air. It swayed alarmingly from side to side as it rose up from the burning platform and drifted majestically across the bleak expanse of the Sargasso Skies.

"We made it!' gasped Trundle, wiping his brow. "By the skin of our teeth!"

9

HAMMERLAND

There was plenty of cheering as the opera house floated away over the heads of the terrified lizards.

A few animals leaned out of the doorways and windows and threw heavy items down on their routed enemies. A few others stamped out the last of the fires. The rest just shouted for joy and hugged one another with relief.

"Well, that's got to be more exciting than any silly old opera!" gasped Esmeralda, a little sooty from the fires but grinning happily as she stood by Trundle at the main entrance.

Jack was just behind them. "Isn't that the *Thief in the Night*?" he said, pointing down to a familiar skyboat caught up in the rigging of a windship wreck.

"By crikey, so it is!" gasped Esmeralda. "Quick, someone—get a rope and a grappling hook. We might just be able to grab it as we go by!"

A rope and a grapple were swiftly found, and Trundle lay on the bottom step of the main entrance, letting the rope down while Esmeralda and Jack sat on him to stop him from being dragged after it. The iron grapple was heavy, and Trundle knew he would have only one chance to hook the little skyboat.

He swung the rope. The grapple hooked on to the raised rear end of the *Thief in the Night* and held fast.

"Secure this end!" shouted Jack. The three of them wound the rope around and around a doorpost.

The rope went taut with a *twoiiinnnngg* sound.

There was a wrenching, screeching noise. Trundle peered down.

"It's working!" he gasped. "She's coming loose!"

With a final twist and quiver, the gallant little skyboat shook herself free of the windship's rigging. Slowly, and with aching muscles, the three friends hauled their in their skyboat and tied her securely to the front steps of the opera house.

"Everything's still safe and sound on board!" said Trundle, wiping his brow. "The crowns are there and everything!"

A low-pitched hooting noise sounded from somewhere above them. A few moments later, the steam moles' iron tug hove into view, black against the gloomy clouds. Ropes came snaking down.

Esmeralda grinned at her friends. "Next stop, Hammerland!" She laughed.

"Next stop, the Crown of Wood!" added Trundle.

"All the same," said Jack, "I hope we get to perform the opera before we have to leave. It'll be such a shame otherwise!"

"So, that's Hammerland," said Trundle. "Odd-looking place, isn't it?"

It had taken two days for the steam moles' steam tug to bring them to the great lump of black and scarred and pock-holed rock that hung below them in the late afternoon sky. And Trundle was right—it did look very odd, indeed. Hundreds of iron pipes and chimneys jutted out of the island, spouting gray and white and black and brown smoke. Here and there, dull steel doors could be seen, set into the black rock, covered in rivets, and from small thick portholes, yellowish lights shone out weakly.

"There are no buildings on the surface at all," puzzled Esmeralda. "Not a one!"

"And I assume those steel rails by the holes are

there to take people inside . . . to where the steam moles must live," said Jack. He shivered. "No. I don't like it. I don't like it at all."

"Where do we start looking for the crown?" wondered Trundle, as downcast by the look of Hammerland as were his companions.

"It's a big place," mused Jack. "Big and dark and dirty and extremely inhospitable."

"We'll work it out," said Esmeralda. "The Fates wouldn't have brought us here if they didn't have *something* in mind."

It had been quite a journey, and it had started in a rather alarming way, as the steam tug had buffeted its way slowly through the endless swirl of winds above the Sargasso Skies. The opera house had sustained some superficial damage, but there had been plenty of time to put things right—and also to fix all the damage done by the invading lizards. The Hernswick Flotilla had joined in, their escape attempt postponed for the time being. With the opera house constantly in view of the clanking steam tug, there was simply no opportunity for them to slip away unnoticed.

Jack had quite enjoyed himself, though. There had been plenty of time for a full dress rehearsal. It had gone quite badly, and Trundle had been horrified by the mayhem and confusion on stage— but then Jack had explained that the worse a dress rehearsal went, the better the actual performance would be.

Trundle had done his best to feel reassured.

As the three friends watched from their vantage point at a window above the main entrance of the opera house, a steam-driven iron windship emerged from a deep hole in the ugly black rock and began its puffing and rumbling way toward them.

"Let's go see what's what," suggested Esmeralda as the windship moored alongside the main entrance and a party of steam moles trudged down the gangplank.

They found the steam moles on stage, speaking with the count.

"Under no circumstances will any of your company be given visas to enter Hammerland," one of the steam moles was saying. "Visitors are not welcome!"

"That's bad," whispered Jack from their hiding place in the wings.

"So how the opera will we perform?" asked the Count.

"The audience will be brought to you," said the steam mole. "Don't worry, your opera house will be packed to the rafters. We steam moles enjoy a good opera, and this will be a sold-out performance."

"Then, most excellent it is!" beamed the Count. "All for the performance is in readiness!"

Trundle, Esmeralda, and Jack got into a worried huddle.

"How are we ever going to find the Crown of Wood if they won't even let us set foot in Hammerland?" asked Trundle.

"Don't fret about it, Trun," said Esmeralda. "The Fates will show us the way when the time comes."

"I rather hope the Fates will leave it till after the performance, if it's all the same to them," said Jack. "I really don't want to miss it—not after all the hard work I've put in." He gazed wistfully down into the orchestra pit. "It was such fun to be among all those musicians, you know." He sighed. "Such fun!"

"You'll get your chance to play, Jack, don't you worry," said Esmeralda. "I have a plan! The audience must be brought here on those iron windships, right?"

"Right," agreed Trundle and Jack.

"And they must be taken away again at the end—on windships," Esmeralda continued. "Which means that all we have to do is disguise ourselves as steam moles and slip aboard a windship at the end of the performance and Bob's your uncle—we're in Hammerland and free to start looking for the jolly old crown." She beamed at her two friends. "What do you say, lads?"

"How exactly do we disguise ourselves as steam moles?" asked Trundle. "Short of shaving our prickles off and painting ourselves black?"

"We just need to borrow three of their leather coats," said Esmeralda. "Buttoned up to our noses and with the collars pulled over our ears, we should just about get away with it, if we keep our heads down."

"I suppose it has to be worth a try," Jack said dubiously. "But it's almost time for a rehearsal, so I'll catch up with your chaps later." He winked. "We're having a few problems with the 'Ride of the Volekyries'—the percussion section always seems to get to the end five bars ahead of the rest of us. Cheerio!" And with a merry wave of his paw, Jack went trotting off to be with his fellow musicians.

Trundle looked at Esmeralda. "He's going to miss all this when we leave," he said.

"He'll get over it," said Esmeralda.

"Hmmm. I wonder if he will . . . ," said Trundle.

The auditorium was packed solid with steam moles—in fact, the audience was so large that the worker animals who had helped to put the opera house together were forced to watch the first-ever performance of *Twilight of the Dogs* from the back and the sides, or from whatever other precarious vantage point they could find.

A hum of expectant pleasure filled the air as Trundle and Esmeralda picked their way to a small empty space at the side of the orchestra pit.

Esmeralda stared at the eagerly waiting steam moles. "They're a strange bunch," she muttered into Trundle's ear.

"You said that about the albinos, too," Trundle whispered back.

"Yes, I know, but I've gotten used to them now." She shook her head. "But these fellows are just plain peculiar, if you ask me."

"No one is asking you," hissed Trundle. "Now pipe down—it's about to start."

Tap. Tap. Tap.

The conductor lifted his baton.

There was a moment of absolute silence. Then the music began.

The rapt audience of steam moles gasped as the curtain rose and Bruinhilda's lofty fortress was revealed among the sharp-edged purple mountains.

Bruinhilda emerged from the wings and swept to center stage.

Before she could even open her mouth, the steam mole audience erupted into titanic applause and cheering and stamping of feet.

"You know something?" Trundle shouted into Esmeralda's ear over the terrific racket that the steam moles were kicking up. "I have the feeling that this will go rather well!"

*F*AREWELL

The opera house shook to the rafters from the rapturous and unending applause of the steam moles. The opera was over and done, but the ecstatic audience would not let the players leave the stage. Five times the curtain had risen and fallen; five times Count Leopold and his performers had joined hands and bowed as the steam moles had cheered and cheered, showering them with an absolute storm of black roses.

And still the clapping and howling and yells of "Bravo" and "Encore" had forced yet another curtain call.

Grinning from ear to ear, and applauding as loudly as anyone, Trundle basked quietly in reflected glory. It would have been nice, he thought, to have been invited up onstage to take his own bow . . . but like Jack had said, backroom boys never get to stand in the limelight. That was just the way things were.

But would the applause never end?

Finally, after so long a time that Trundle's paws ached and his ears were ringing, the ovation began to fade away.

Count Leopold leaned toward them from the stage. "You must up here coming be!" he shouted. "We are for those who helpful have been, a celebration having! Come, Ermintruda—come also, my spiky little chap. Join us! Join us!"

"Esmeralda!" shouted Esmeralda. "How many more times?" But she grabbed Trundle by the arm and dragged him up onto the crowded stage.

"But we have to steal leather coats and mingle with the steam moles," Trundle reminded her.

"Plenty of time for that!" Esmeralda declared. "I'm not missing out on a party!"

And what a party it was! Everyone was there—the worker animals, the performers, every single member of the orchestra—all talking loudly at the same time and congratulating one another and leaping up and down around the count while he smiled and bowed and said thank you in his roundabout and upside-down kind of way.

"Thank you I do!" he said over and over. "My heart's bottom you all thank!"

And then Jack struck up a cheery dance tune on his rebec and several other members of the orchestra joined in, and soon an impromptu dance was taking place, all the animals twining in and around one another, albino and captive, Hernswick Hounds and performers arm in arm with Trundle and Esmeralda.

"This is more like it!" croaked Hopper, whirling past Trundle and Esmeralda with Sheila the stoat in his arms. "Music you can shake a leg to!"

And much as he had enjoyed the opera, Trundle couldn't help but agree with him.

It was not until some time later that Trundle staggered out of the heaving throng to take a quick breather. He sat on the edge of the stage, panting for breath. He mopped his brow and gazed out over the empty auditorium. Through the open front doors of the opera house, he saw the last of the steam mole windships chugging off.

"No!" he groaned. "Oh, no!"

Not a single steam mole was left in the opera

house. They had been so engrossed in the festivities, they had totally missed their chance to slip away.

He got to his feet and went in search of Esmeralda.

Before he found her, the count stopped the music and called for quiet.

"I have an announcement!" he boomed as the people gathered around him. "I know some of you here against your will were kept. And for that I me apologize! But for high art, must sacrifices made have to be! Without your help, willing or unwilling, not have this done I could. But a great success have been we! And this say I to you now—for any of you who with the opera to stay wish, will I a warm welcome extend! And payment will I you also give!"

There was a general gasp and a murmur of surprised voices.

Count Leopold spread his great paws again. "But for those who rather home go would—then take you my blessings with you!" He wiped a tear from his eye.

"I will ever your grateful friend be!"

There was some cheering and quite a lot of overlapping conversations as the newly liberated workers discussed their options. Trundle got the impression from what he could hear that although most wanted to go home, a few seemed happy to stay on.

Esmeralda came strolling up. "Well, that was a great party, wasn't it?" she said. "Did you see those albinos dance? They might seem a bit subdued and standoffish to begin with, but they're real party animals once you get to know them." She frowned. "And why do you have a face on you like a torn omelet, Trundle?"

"The steam moles have all gone," he informed her.

"Oh, rats!" she said. "We'll have to think of a different way of getting to Hammerland. Perhaps under cover of darkness, we can fly the *Thief in the Night* over there?"

"Perhaps," Trundle said, unconvinced. "But . . ."

He was interrupted by one of the performers—an elderly beaver, who had played the part of the king of the noble bears.

"Ah, my dear little chap," hooted the beaver. "Just the very fellow! Would you be a dear and put these things away in the props room for me?" And so saying, he bundled his crown and his orb and scepter into Trundle's arms and flounced off to chat with the count and some other cast members.

"What a nerve!" declared Trundle.

"Oh, let's just get rid of them," said Esmeralda. She frowned at the crown. "Look at that!" she exclaimed crossly. "He's torn the silver paper off a couple of the prongs!"

Trundle looked at the brown prongs revealed by the stripped-back silver foil. "This crown is made of wood!" He snorted. "And the way things are going, this is the only wooden crown we're going to get our hands on!"

They found the props master and asked him

where the King's adornments should be put.

"The crown goes in a box on the second shelf at the back of the props room," they were told. "In among some other things that we salvaged off a wrecked old wind galleon. You can't miss the box—it has the words *Five of Six* engraved on the lid."

"Thanks," said Trundle, leading the way off the stage and through the wings to the props room.

"Um . . . Trundle . . . ," Esmeralda said as she trotted along after him, plucking at his tunic.

"What is it now?" Trundle snapped tetchily. "Some brilliant new scheme for getting us into Hammerland? A giant catapult to fire us there, perhaps?"

"*Five of Six!*" yelled Esmeralda. "The box has *Five of Six* written on it! And the props master said they found it on an old wind galleon! Doesn't that ring any bells with you, Trundle?"

"Not particularly," said Trundle as he passed

between the racks of stage clothes and came to the row of shelves at the back of the room.

"Oh, you witless hedgehog!" gasped Esmeralda. "There are times when I really despair of you!"

"If you say so," grumbled Trundle, still out of sorts that they had missed their best chance of getting to Hammerland.

"Where do you think that crown you are holding comes from, Trundle?" asked Esmeralda, barely keeping her temper with him. *"Originally,* I mean?"

"How should I know?" muttered Trundle. He spotted the wooden box with *Five of Six* engraved on the lid. With a disgruntled grunt, he opened the box. A brown and cracked square of parchment was glued inside the lid.

He glanced at it without much interest, but went suddenly rigid to the very tips of his prickles, his eyes as round as the Bear King's orb.

This is what he read:

Ye players of the ancient game

Who plot y'r course with might and main

Shall all the crowns unite again

Among the stones of Trembling Plain.

Then ye who would the badgers' cause abet

Fly swift and true toward Sunsett.

"Th-th-this *here* is the Crown of Wood?" Trundle gabbled, staring at the silver-coated crown in his paws. "The real thing? The actual Crown of Wood we're looking for?"

"The penny drops at last!" said Esmeralda, chuckling. "Yes, Trundle my lad! This here is the ancient Crown of Wood from the prophecy."

"We had it with us all along?" groaned Trundle.

"It looks like it."

With shaking paws, Trundle stripped away the

rest of the silver foil, revealing a plain but really rather elegant wooden crown

"Hello, you fellows," said Jack. "I've been looking all over for you." He smiled uneasily at them. "I have something I need to tell you . . . something rather . . ." His eyes almost popped out as he saw the Crown of Wood, the box, and the scrap of brown parchment with the clue on it.

"Is . . . is . . . that . . . what I think . . . it is . . . ?" he gasped, quite taken aback.

"It is!" Trundle laughed. "Would you believe it?"

"Well, no, not really," said Jack. "That's marvelous!"

"Do you have any idea what the clue might mean, Jack?" Esmeralda asked.

Jack looked more closely at the parchment and shook his head. "Sorry, I don't," he said. "I'd guess that Trembling Plain must be a place somewhere. And 'Sunsett' is spelled with two Ts at the end—which might be significant, or might not."

"We should go back to Widdershins and show it to Percy," said Trundle. "If anyone can explain the rhyme, I'm betting he can! After all, he helped us find the Crown of Iron."

"And he's looking after two of the crowns for us," added Esmeralda. "So we ought to go see him anyway. Widdershins ho, my lads! Trundle, pop the crown in its box and we'll slip away before anyone realizes we've gone!" She grinned widely. "All aboard the *Thief in the Night!*"

"Um, listen, you fellows," Jack said, looking awkward. "The thing is, I was rather intending to stay on with the count for a while." He looked appealingly at them. "If that's okay with you fellows, of course. I don't want to let anyone down." He gave them a weak grin. "You don't mind, do you? I mean, questing with you chaps has been marvelous, truly it has—but at heart I'll always be a musician, you know."

Trundle and Esmeralda looked at each other, shocked and dismayed by their friend's announcement.

"Of . . . of course we don't mind," gulped Esmeralda at last.

"A chap's got to do what a chap's got to do," added Trundle. "We quite understand!"

"And after all," Jack said, with a tear in his eye, "that Badger Block prophecy only mentioned the Lamplighter and the Princess in Darkness. It didn't say anything about a traveling troubadour."

"Listen," Esmeralda said, her voice choking. "I'm not a big one for long good-byes. Let's just shake paws right here and now, and then we'll go."

But Jack wasn't having any of that. He hugged them both until they could hardly breathe.

"Best of luck," he said, wiping tears out of his eyes. "And we'll meet again one day—I'm certain of it!"

With that, he turned and walked quickly away.

Trundle blew his nose loudly.

"Well," said Esmeralda. "That's that, then!" She wiped her sleeve across her snout. "Looks like it's just you and me again, Trun! Let's get out of here."

A few minutes later, they were aboard the *Thief in the Night*.

Esmeralda was at the tiller. The sails were up and billowing. Trundle loosened the mooring ropes. The little skyboat bobbed and the sails caught the wind.

"Bye, Jack," murmured Trundle as the skyboat skipped away. "Goodbye, my friend!"

With a heavy sigh, he turned his eyes away from the opera house.

"Cheer up, Trun," said Esmeralda, her eyes shining with excitement. "Don't you realize what this means? We're off in search of the very last crown! The quest is almost over!"

A smile touched the corner of Trundle's snout. "And then we can go home!" he said. "But . . . do you know something, Es? I'm not at all sure I *want* to go home!"

"That's the spirit, my lad!" Esmeralda laughed. "Here's to new skies, new islands, and new adventures!"

"Yes! To new adventures!" Trundle echoed happily as an especially playful gust of wind caught the *Thief in the Night* and sent her skimming away through the starry sky.